George Du Maurier

Pictures of English society

George Du Maurier

Pictures of English society

ISBN/EAN: 9783741194184

Manufactured in Europe, USA, Canada, Australia, Japa

Cover: Foto ©Andreas Hilbeck / pixelio.de

Manufactured and distributed by brebook publishing software
(www.brebook.com)

George Du Maurier

Pictures of English society

Pictures of

English Society.

No. IV.

The Parchment Paper Series.

A Disenchantment.

VERY UNSOPHISTICATED OLD LADY (*from the extremely remote country*). "*Dear* me! He's a *very* different-looking Person from what I had always imagined!"

Pictures of
English Society

BY

GEORGE DU MAURIER.

FROM "PUNCH."

NEW YORK:

D. Appleton & Co., 1, 3, & 5 Bond Street.

1884.

George du Maurier.

GEORGE DU MAURIER, as we learn from an article in THE CENTURY MAGAZINE of May last, written by Mr. Henry James, was born in England, of a French father and an English mother. He was taken to France in his early years, and educated there; later he returned to England, where he has since resided. He gave no early evidence of the remarkable talent which has made him world-famous, and was educated for a chemist. He had no inclination for this science, although he came to have a laboratory of his own; but a passion for art had now become awakened, and his laboratory was converted into a studio. He studied art at Paris and at Düsseldorf, but suddenly, without warning, a great calamity befell him. His eye-sight became so seriously affected that he was obliged for a time to abandon all work.

George du Maurier.

"He was condemned," says Mr. James, "to many dark days, at the end of which he learned that he should have to do his work for the rest of his life with less than half a man's portion of the sense most valuable to the artist." But for this misfortune the world would probably be admiring Du Maurier as a painter of GENRE subjects rather than simply as a draughtsman in black and white.

The earliest sketch, according to Mr. James, contributed by Du Maurier to "Punch," appeared in the number for December 5, 1863, now just twenty years ago. John Leech died in October, 1864, and soon thereafter the hand of Du Maurier became frequently apparent on the pages of that comic journal. "The finish and delicacy, the real elegance of these early drawings," says Mr. James, "are extreme; the hand was already the hand of a brilliant executant." The larger part of Du Maurier's work has been done for "Punch," but he has designed many illustrations for books. He has been a regular contributor to the "Cornhill," his first work for that magazine being a

2

series of designs for Mrs. Gaskell's "Wives and Daughters." In 1868 he made a number of drawings for a new edition of Thackeray's "Esmond," which are considered among the most charming of his book illustrations.

It is certainly remarkable that "Punch" should have been so fortunate as to find as a successor to the inimitable John Leech an artist no less admirable and inimitable. It is not too much to say that the principal attraction of "Punch" for many readers has been the exquisite social satires from the pencil of Du Maurier. There is nothing comparable with them elsewhere. Du Maurier's fineness of perception, to quote from Mr. James, his remarkable power of specifying types, his taste, his grace, his lightness, and an indescribable refinement in his art, are due possibly to a Gallic element in his nature, but they are essentially English in spirit and thought. English life and character have never been more faithfully depicted, never presented with keener insight into peculiarities of types either by English novelists or artists ; and this striking fact gives to Du Maurier's drawings a permanent charm wholly independent of their humorous or satirical element. He gives us most delightful young women, and sketches of young Englishmen that are as accurate as photographs; and his portraits of all the various social grades are wonderfully to the life. " The pretty points of children," quoting again from Mr. James, "are intimately known to him ; he understands, moreover, the infant wardrobe as well as the infant mind. His little boys and girls are 'turned out' with a completeness which has made the despair of many an American mother." As Pictures of English Society, therefore, his drawings are a lasting study. They reveal the current "craze"; they show the tendencies of social refinement; they indicate social usage; they open to the foreigner the English drawing-room, the English nursery, the English playground; they show us the amusements, the ambitions, the aptitudes, and many of the virtues as well as the foibles of that remarkable people.

4

Contents.

Contents.

Contents.

Contents.

Pictures of English Society.

A Venial Misuse.

A Venial Mistake.

NEW BEAUTY (*unversed as yet in the mysteries of High Life*). "Who's that wonderful Old Gentleman?"

THE CAPTAIN. "Sir Digby de Rigby, a Hampshire Baronet; one of the oldest in England; James the First's creation, you know."

NEW BEAUTY (*determined to be surprised at nothing*). "Indeed! How well preserved he is! I shouldn't have thought him more than Seventy or Eighty!"

Terrible Result of the Higher Education of Women!

Miss HYPATIA JONES, Spinster of Arts (on her way to Refreshment), informs Professor PARALLAX, F. R. S., that "Young Men do very well to Look at, or to Dance with, or even to Marry, and all that kind of Thing!" but that "as to enjoying any Rational Conversation with any Man under Fifty, *that* is *completely* out of the Question!"

A Motherly Puff.

MANŒUVRING MAMMA (*anxious that her Daughter's chief attraction should not escape the notice of the very eligible Young Man who is taking her—the Daughter—down to supper*). "Maria! Maria!!"

MARIA. "Yes, Mamma!"

MANŒUVRING MAMMA (*in loud whisper*). "Take your Eye-lashes out of Tangle, Darling!"

Fashionable Execution.

Fashionable Emulation.

LADY (*speaking with difficulty*). "What have you made it round the Waist, Mrs. Price?"

DRESSMAKER. "Twenty-one Inches, Ma'am. You couldn't *breathe* with less!"

LADY. "What's Lady Jemima Jones's Waist?"

DRESSMAKER. "Nineteen-and-a-half just now, Ma'am. But her Ladyship's a head shorter than you are, and she's got ever so much thinner since her Illness last Autumn!"

LADY. "Then make it *Nineteen*, Mrs. Price, and *I'll* engage to get into it!"

17

Al Madame. A Régent's Villégani . Birmą.

18

At Madame Aldegond's (Regent Street).

FIRST DRESSMAKER. "Do you—a—wear Chamois-leather Underclothing?"

NEW CUSTOMER. "No; certainly not!"

FIRST DRESSMAKER. "Oh! then pray take a Seat, and I will send the *Second* Dressmaker!"

"Noblesse Oblige"

20

"Noblesse Oblige."

INTERLOCUTOR. "Who's that showy Woman who Talks and Laughs so loud, and digs People in the Ribs?"

INTERLOCUTRIX. "Oh, that's the Duchess of Bayswater. She was a Lady Gwendolen Beaumanoir, you know!"

INTERLOCUTOR (*with warmth*). "Ah! to be sure! That accounts for her high-bred Ease, her aristocratic Simplicity of Manner, her natural and straightforward——"

INTERLOCUTRIX (*putting up her eye-glass*). "By the bye, pardon me! I have unintentionally misinformed you: it's Mrs. Judkins. She's the Widow of an Alderman, and her Father was a Cheesemonger in the New Cut!"

INTERLOCUTOR. "*Dear* me!—Ah!—Hum!—er—Hum!—Ha! That *quite* alters the case! How she goes on, to be sure! I wonder she's admitted into decent society!"

[N. B.—*It was the Duchess, after all.*

21

An Incomplete Amusement

22

An Incomplete Amusement.

THE SQUIRE. "Well, Mossoo le Barrong, how did you like the Meet of the Queen's Hounds this Morning?"

DISTINGUISHED FRENCHMAN. "O ver much! Ze Paysage it vos beautiful; ze Ladies, zey vare sharmeengs; and ze Costumes vare adorables! But——zare vos no Promenade!——no Band of Music!——Nossing!"

A Slight Misunderstanding.

24

A Slight Misunderstanding.

" Do you evah *Wink*, Miss Evangeline?"

" Do I ever *what*, Mr. Smythe?"

" *Wink?*"

" What *do* you mean, Sir?"

" Well, *Skate*, if you pwefer the Expwession!"

A Sitting Gobba.

26

A Rising Genius.

YOUNG LADY (*in course of conversation*). "You've read 'Pendennis,' of course?"

FASHIONABLE SCRIBBLER (*who is, however, quite unknown to fame*). "A—'Pendennis'! Ah!—let me see! That's Thackeray's, isn't it? No, I've not. The fact is, I never read Books—I *write* them!"

Medical Section.

28

Musical Egotism.

HERR MAESTRO (*who has been indulging the Company with two Masses, three Symphonies, a dozen Impromptus, and a few other little things of his own*). "Vill you not now Zing zomzing, Miss Anchelica?"

MISS ANGELICA (*with diffidence, pulling off her gloves*). "H'm! —H'm!—I'm afraid I'm a little Hoarse to-day; but if——"

HERR MAESTRO (*with alacrity*). "Ach sôh! In zat case I vill not bress you. I haf gombôset a Zonata in F moll—shall I blay it for you? Yes?"

[*Proceeds to do so.*

29

A Sensitive Plant

A Sensitive Plant.

(*Herr* PUMPERNICKEL, *having just played a Composition of his own, bursts into tears.*)

CHORUS OF FRIENDS. "Oh, *what* is the matter? What can we do for you?"

HERR PUMPERNICKEL. "Ach! nossing! nossing! Bot ven I hear really *cool* Music, zen must I always *veep!*"

Awkward.

ALGERNON FITZTOPSAWYER (*who has not caught his Partner's name*). "Are you—a—going to the 'Pigstye'?"

HIS PARTNER (*by name 'Miss Hogge', whose parents are about to give a great Ball*). "Oh, yes! I am One of the Litter!"

The Busines of Pleasure.

34

The Business of Pleasure.

PROFESSOR GUZZLETON (*to Fair Chatterbox*). "Are you aware that our Host has a French Cook?"

FAIR CHATTERBOX. "So I hear!"

PROFESSOR GUZZLETON. "And that that French Cook is the best in London?"

FAIR CHATTERBOX. "So I believe!"

PROFESSOR GUZZLETON. "Then don't you think we had better defer all further Conversation till we meet again in the Drawing-room?"

36

Veto.

"SHALL we—a—Sit down?"

"I should like to; but my Dressmaker says I mustn't!"

37

An Alternative

38

An Alternative.

(*Time*, 9 *P. M.*)

"CHARLES, Love, Lady LEDBURY is at Home to-night, and Mrs. GELASMA has a Concert, and there's the Duchess of IPSWICH's Dance. Now, are we going to these Places, or not? For if we *are*, it is Time for me to go and dress; and if we are *not*, it is Time for me to put a Mustard-Plaster on my Chest, some Flannel round my Throat, and go straight off to Bed!"

A Damper.

BONIFACE BRASENOSE (*an amiable but æsthetic youth, exhibiting his Art-treasures*). "That's—a—a—Mother and Child, a—a—Fifteenth Century——"

FASHIONABLE LADY. "I should have thought it earlier!"

BONIFACE BRASENOSE. "A—may I ask why?"

FASHIONABLE LADY. "Oh, I should have thought they could Paint better than that, so late as the Fifteenth Century!"

Episode in Pigm Life.

Episode in High Life.

(*From* OUR JEAMES's *Sketch-book*.)

THE LADY KEROSINE DE COLZA. "I can not tell you how pleased I am to meet You here, Dr. Blenkinsop, and especially to go down to Dinner with you."

DR. BLENKINSOP (*an eminent Physician, much pleased*). "You flatter me, I'm sure, Lady Kerosine!"

LADY KEROSINE. "Oh, no! It's so nice to sit by Some-body who can tell one exactly what to Eat, Drink, and Avoid, you know!"

Beauty a Critic on Beauty.

FRED AND CHARLIE. "There's Mrs. Spiffington! *Ain't* she looking Lovely!"

MRS. BILLINGTON (*a rival Beauty*). "I never *could* see the Loveliness of Mrs. Spiffington, I confess! Now, that *short* Woman, with the large Black Hat, who's with her, *is* Lovely, if you like!"

45

Ringleass Charlie.

46

Misplaced Charity.

On coming out of Church, General Sir TALBOT DE LA POER SANGRAZUL is so struck by the beauty of the Afternoon Sky, that he forgets to put on his Hat, and Lady JONES (who is rather near-sighted) drops a Penny into it.

A Man's Revise.

48

A Man's Revenge.

OUR Gallant, though middle-aged, Friend, has great pleasure in introducing his *Second* Love (whom he is going to Marry next Week) to his *First* (who jilted him just a quarter of a century ago).

Alexsis Scarelli.

50

Alarming Scarcity.

(SCENE—*Club Smoking-Room.*)

FIRST YOUNG SWELL. "Aw!—going anywhere?"

SECOND DITTO. "No!—asked to ten 'Hops' to-night! The Idea has completely floored me!"

THIRD DITTO. "By Jove! I've been thinking of letting myself out at Ten Pounds a Night. A Fellow might recoup himself for a bad Book on the Derby."

Pudding Club.

Wedding Gifts.

BRIDE. "Oh, Mamma!—see what's just come!"

MAMMA. "Charming!—how kind of them! Who sent it?"

BRIDE. "Oh, I didn't look. But it makes No. 248!"

SISTER (*who is writing out the list of presents*). "249. Darling; 248 came just after Lunch!"

53

Refinements of Modern Speech.

54

Refinements of Modern Speech.

(SCENE—*A Drawing-Room in "Passionate Brompton."*)

FAIR ÆSTHETIC (*suddenly, and in the deepest tones, to Smith, who has just been introduced to take her in to Dinner*). " Are you *Intense ?* "

Feline Amenities.

"By the bye, Clara, I expect a great Friend of mine this Afternoon—Major Miniver."

"Horrid Man! I can't bear him."

"And *why*, pray?"

"Because I know he *Hates* me!"

"Does he, really? I thought he scarcely *Knew you!*"

57

Festive Housekeeping

Festive Housekeeping.

DAUGHTER OF THE HOUSE (*to her Cousin*). "Haven't you been down to Supper before, Charles? I ask because we have only reckoned for One Supper each!"

[CHARLES *has not yet touched a morsel, but his Fair Companion is coming down to supper for the Third time. Let us hope she takes the hint.*]

A Flower of Fashion.

A Flower of Fashion.

FASHIONABLE MILLINER. "You'll have the Flower on the *Left* Side of the Bonnet, of *course*, Madam?"

FASHIONABLE LADY. "Well—er—No! The Fact is, there's a Pillar on the Left Side of my Pew in Church, so that only the *Right* Side of my Head is seen by the Congregation. Of course I could change my Pew!"

FASHIONABLE LADY'S HUSBAND. "Ya-as. Or even the Church, you know, if necessary."

[Fashionable Milliner considers the point.

Drawing-Room Minstrels.

Drawing-Room Minstrels.

(What they have to put up with sometimes.)

AFFABLE DUCHESS *(to Amateur Tenor, who has just been warbling M. Gounod's last).* "Charming! Charming! Charming! You must really get Somebody to introduce you to me!"

The Waning of the Honeymoon.

The Waning of the Honeymoon.

ANGELINA (*suppressing an inclination to yawn*). "How nice it would be if some Friend were to turn up; wouldn't it, Edwin?"

EDWIN (*after yawning elaborately*). "Ye-e-s!—or even some Enemy!"

Hypercriticism.

GRACE (*whispering*). " What lovely Boots your Partner's got, Mary ! "

MARY (*ditto*). " Yes, unfortunately he shines at the Wrong End."

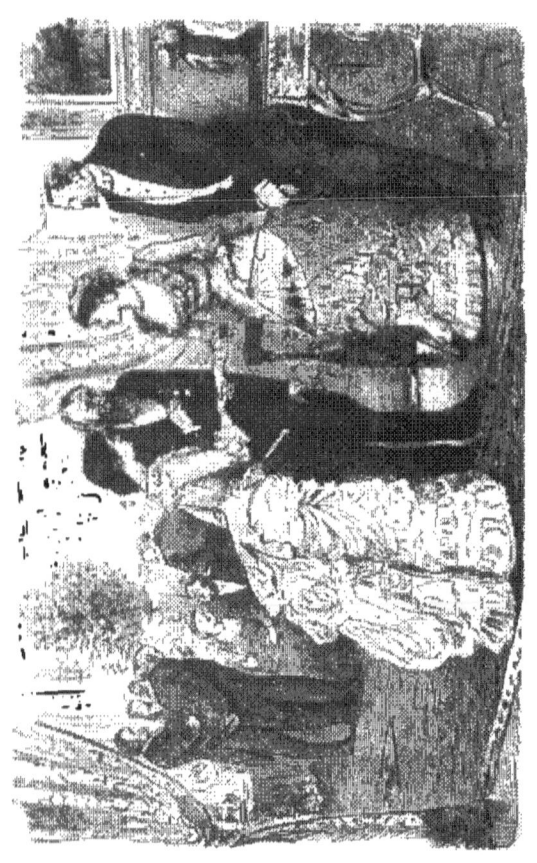

68

Things one would rather have left Unsaid.

AMIABLE HOSTESS. "What! must you go already? Really, Professor, it's too bad of this sweet young Wife of yours to carry you off so early! She always does!"

PROFESSOR. "No, no, not *always*, Mrs. Bright! At *most* Houses I positively have to *drag her away!*"

Music at Home.

JONES (*an eligible Bachelor, whispering tenderly*). "There's too much Music in this world, Miss Mary! I should have been Married long ago, if it hadn't been for too much Music! Whenever I'd screwed up my Pluck to the pitch of Popping the Question, somebody always began to Sing, and of course I had to——"

CHORUS OF BYSTANDERS. "SHSHSHSHSH!"

[*Poor Jones is frustrated for the twelfth time!*

82

Instinctive Gratitude.

MAUD (*an Aristocratic Child*). "How Pretty and Clever you are, Mother! I'm *so* glad you Married into our family!"

73

74

It's not so Difficult to Speak French, after all.

MISTRESS (*fluently*). "Oh—er—Françoise, il faut que vous alliez chez le Chemist, dans High Street, pour le Gargle de Mademoiselle Maud; et chez le Toy-Shop, pour le Lawn-Tennis Bat de Monsieur Malcolm; et n'oubliez pas mon Waterproof, chez le Cleaner, vis-à-vis l'Underground Railway Station; et dites à Smithson, le Builder (dans Church Lane à côté du Public-house, vous savez), que le Kitchen-Boiler est—est—est——"

FRANÇOISE (*who has been longer in England than her new Mistress thinks*). "Est Burrrst! Très bien, Madame."

A Retort Courteous.

NEW PARLOR-MAID. "Here's a Letter Ma'am, if you please!"

NEW MISTRESS. "Pray, Mary, are you not accustomed to see Letters handed on a Tray?"

NEW PARLOR-MAID. "Yes, Ma'am. But I didn't know *you was!*"

78

Catching a Weasel Asleep.

MRS. PONSONBY DE TOMKYNS (*pointing to her books*). "They are not *many*, Lord Adolphus, but they are all *Friends*—dear Old Friends !"

NOBLE POET (*taking down a Volume of his own Poems and finding the leaves uncut*). "Ah ! hum ! I'm glad to find that you don't *cut* all your Old Friends, Mrs. de Tomkyns !"

[*Mrs. P. de T. is at a loss for once.*

Induction.

SYLVIA. "There go Uncle George, and Aunt Mary, and the Baby! What a Fuss they make about that Baby, to be sure!"

DAISY. "People always make a Fuss about their First-born, and always have ever since the World began."

SYLVIA. "I don't suppose Adam and Eve made much Fuss about Cain."

DAISY. "Why not?"

SYLVIA. "Well, they'd never seen a Baby before, and must have thought him quite an Idiot!"

82

A Fashionable Complaint.

MAMMA. "Papa dear, the Children have been asked to the Howard Willoughby Robinsons' on the Eleventh, the Howard Willoughby Robinsons' on the Eleventh, the Talbot Brownes's on Jones's on the Fifteenth, and the Talbot Brownes's on the Twenty-first. They'll be dreadfully disappointed if you don't let them go! May I write and accept, dear Papa?"

DEAR PAPA (*savagely*). "Oh, just as you please! But, as Juvenile Parties should always be taken in time, you had better write to Dr. Squills too, and tell him to call on the Twelfth, Sixteenth, and Twenty-second."

Things one would wish to have-Expressed Differently.

MUSICAL MAIDEN. "I hope I am not boring you, Playing so much?"

ENAMORED YOUTH. "Oh, no! Pray go on! I—I'd so much sooner hear you Play than talk!"

Perplexing—Very!

"My *dear* Eliza, Sir Arthur Pillington is the Man for *your* Complaint. *So* clever, and a *perfect* Gentleman. *Pray* send for him!"

"Sir Arthur Pillington, indeed! Why, he nearly killed an Aunt of mine! Send for Wilfrid Jones, Eliza. *Trust* me, there's *nobody* like him. He listens to every symptom!"

"No, no, Eliza. Listen to *me*. I know a little Man in Hammersmith, who saved my poor Grandmother's life when every other Doctor had——,"

"Hammersmith! Nonsense! I don't believe in *any* English Doctors! Let me bring Herr *Schwartzmüller* to you, my dear Eliza. He——,"

"My *dear* Eliza, *have* you lived all these years without knowing that Dr. Thrupp Robinson, the Homœopathic Allopath, in Bermondsey, is the *only* Physician in London who——," &c., &c., &c.

Circumstantial Evidence.

"WHO's that frizzly black-haired Woman talking to my Husband on the Ottoman?"

"She's a Mrs. CADOGAN SMYTHE."

"Indeed! She's good at Flattering People, I should say : and knows how to lay it on pretty thick !"

"Ah! you infer that, no doubt, from her Attitude and Expression?"

"Oh dear, no! From my Husband's !"

89

Bachelor Bluff:

His Opinions, Sentiments, and Disputations. By Oliver B. Bunce.

The Rhymester;
Or, *The Rules of Rhyme*.

A Guide to English Versification. With a Dictionary of Rhymes, an Examination of Classical Measures, and Comments upon Burlesque, Comic Verse, and Song-Writing. By the late TOM HOOD. Edited, with Additions, by ARTHUR PENN.

Three whole chapters have been added to the work by the American editor—one on the sonnet, one on the *rondeau* and the *ballade*, and a third on other fixed forms of verse ; while he has dealt freely with the English author's text, making occasional alterations, frequent insertions, and revising the dictionary of rhymes.

" Its chapters relate to matters of which the vast majority of those who write verses are utterly ignorant, and yet which no poet, however brilliant, should neglect to learn. Though rules can never teach the art of poetry, they may serve to greatly mitigate the evils of ordinary versification. This instructive treatise contains a dictionary of rhymes, an examination of classical measures, and comments on various forms of verse-writing. We earnestly commend this little book to all those who have thoughts which can not be expressed except in poetic measures."—*New York Observer.*

" If young writers will only get the book and profit by its instructions, editors throughout the English-speaking world will unite in thanking this author for his considerate labor."—*New York Home Journal.*

18mo, cloth, extra. Uniform with " The Orthoëpist " and " The Verbalist." Price, $1.00.

New York : D. APPLETON & CO., 1, 3, & 5 Bond Street.

Social Etiquette
of New York.

CONTENTS:

The Value of Etiquette; Introductions; Solicitations;
Strangers in Towns; Débuts in Society; Visiting, and Visiting Cards for Ladies; Card and Visiting Customs for Gen-
tlemen; Morning Receptions and Kettle-Drums; Giving
and attending Parties, Balls, and Germans; Dinner-giving
and Dining out; Breakfasts, Luncheons, and Suppers;
Opera and Theatre Parties, Private Theatricals, and Musi-
cales; Extended Visits; Customs and Costumes at Thea-
tres, Concerts, and Operas (being two additional chapters
written for this edition); Etiquette of Weddings (rewritten,
for this edition, in accordance with the latest fashionable
usage); Christenings and Birthdays; Marriage Anniversa-
ries; New Year's Day in New York; Funeral Customs and
Seasons of Mourning.

18mo, cloth, gilt, price, $1.00.

New York: D. APPLETON & CO., 1, 3, & 5 Bond Street.